DO CATS HAVE NINE LIVES?

A Question of Science Book

DO CATS HAVE NINE LIVES?

The strange things people say
about animals around the house

by Deborah Dennard
illustrated by Jackie Urbanovic

Carolrhoda Books, Inc. / Minneapolis

Each word that appears in **BOLD** in the text is explained in the glossary on page 32.

LIBRARY OF CONGRESS CATALOGING-IN-PUBLICATION DATA

Dennard, Deborah.
   Do cats have nine lives? : the strange things people say about animals
around the house / by Deborah Dennard ; illustrated by Jackie Urbanovic.
      p.   cm. – (A Question of science book)
   Summary: Questions and answers examine and explain common mis-
conceptions about familiar animals.
   ISBN 0-87614-720-1 (lib. bdg.)
   1. Animals—Miscellanea—Juvenile literature. 2. Domestic animals—
Miscellanea—Juvenile literature. [1. Animals—Miscellanea. 2. Questions
and answers.] I. Urbanovic, Jackie, ill. II. Title. III. Series.
QL49.D426 1993
591–dc20   92-10353
                                                                CIP
                                                                AC

Manufactured in the United States of America

1 2 3 4 5 6 98 97 96 95 94 93

For Robert, Audrey and Berkleigh—*D.D.*
To my favorite beast—*J.U.*

Do cats have nine lives?

Do mice really like cheese?

And can squirrels fly?

If you think you know the answers, think again.
People say the strangest things about animals around
the house. You can't believe all that you hear.

Let's take a look at some of the things people believe
about animals. Will you agree?

Cats are daring animals, but do they really have nine lives?

A cat leaps from a second floor window and lands on its paws. Another cat shoots across the street, just missing a passing car. Cats survive by moving quickly and gracefully. They are often very lucky, but they don't have extra lives.

Do cats use magic tricks to catch their **prey**?

If you've ever watched a cat try to catch a bird or a
squirrel, you may have thought the cat was a magician.
A hungry cat sitting at the base of a tree can sometimes
trick its prey into thinking it isn't hunting at all. If a
bird or squirrel doesn't notice the cat, it could become
lunch! Our cats are good hunters, but they're not
magicians.

Do mice really like cheese?

Mice often live where people live. They eat whatever
food people leave around the house—including cheese.
But cheese is not their favorite snack. Most mice
like seeds, oats, and peanuts better than cheese.

People say you should never touch a baby bird, because its mother won't like your smell on her baby. Do you think that's true?

It's a good story and one that many people believe. But most birds have no sense of smell. A mother bird probably can't smell your smell, or any smell, on her baby.

You still shouldn't touch a baby bird, and here's why. When you find a baby bird out of its nest, it's probably just learning to fly. If you move the baby, its mother won't know where to find it. Mother bird is probably close by, waiting to feed her baby.

Most birds have no sense of smell, but there are some exceptions. Kiwi birds from New Zealand use their long bills to smell worms and insects underground. Seagulls called fulmars may be able to smell fish in the ocean. And vultures may be able to smell rotting meat. Scientists still have a lot to learn about birds and their sense of smell.

Are raccoons so neat and clean they even wash their paws before dinner?

Maybe you've see a raccoon take food from a garbage can. A raccoon will often carry the food to water to splash it about. It may look as if the raccoon is washing its paws, but it's really doing something else.

In the wild, raccoons use their paws to catch frogs and crayfish in the water. When they "wash" food from garbage cans, they are just going through the motions of hunting at the water's edge.

Can pet parrots talk?

Parrots copy sounds, all kinds of sounds—words, whistles, buzzers, bells, songs, and alarms. Parrots don't understand what they hear and say. Have you ever tried talking to a parrot? If you have, you know that parrots only repeat things they've heard before. They can't put words together to make new sentences.

People often say that toads cause warts.
What do you think?

Toads have bumpy, warty-looking skin. Inside the
bumps is a poison that makes toads taste bad to their
predators, other animals that might eat toads. Wash
your hands after touching a toad—because of the
poison, not because of warts. Warts, like colds, are
caused by **viruses,** not by toads!

Are worms too icky and slimy to be animals?

Animals are living things that breathe, eat food, drink water, and have babies. Even worms are animals. There are many more worms, bugs, and other creepy-crawly creatures in the world than all the soft, furry animals put together!

Worms are slimy for a very good reason. Their slime
helps them take oxygen from the air right into their
bodies. Worms could not live without their slime.

Some people think squirrels can fly. Do you think so too?

The gray, brown, or red squirrels you see outside are good jumpers, but they can't fly. Some other very small squirrels have long flaps of skin between their front and back feet. They are called flying squirrels. But even flying squirrels cannot really fly. Instead, they glide. Spreading their legs apart, they jump from a tree branch. Their flaps of skin act like little parachutes.

Flying squirrels live over much of North America in places where there are big trees. You may even have flying squirrels in your backyard. But because flying squirrels are small and **nocturnal**—coming out only at night—you will probably never see them.

Do cats and dogs fight like cats and dogs?

They don't have to. Cats and dogs are not natural
enemies. They just need to get to know each other.
Dogs may chase cats that are strangers. Cats may
scratch dogs they don't know. But dogs and cats that
live together can become best friends.

Are dogs really our *best friends?*

Our dogs can be our friends, sometimes our best friends. They help protect our homes. Some dogs herd, fetch, or hunt for us. And some dogs just cuddle. Dogs can give people love and help.

The same is true for all **domestic** animals. Guide dogs, house cats, pet parakeets, and horses are all domestic animals. These animals give people love or work or help. In return, we give them food, safety, and friendship.

Can wild animals become good pets?

Lions, monkeys, raccoons, and other wild animals are *wild*, just as the name suggests. They live on their own away from people. They find their own food and shelter. Wild animals don't make good pets, because they can never really be tamed. Inside themselves, they will always be wild.

So, are black cats bad luck?

Does Polly really want a cracker?

And will a lost dog always find its way home?

If you think you know the answers, remember, animals aren't always as they seem. There are many things we don't know about animals, even the animals we live with every day. To find out which animal stories are true and which are just tall tales, keep asking questions! The answers are sure to surprise you.

GLOSSARY

domestic: Animals that have been changed by people so they can live with and work for people. Farm animals—chickens, cows, goats, pigs, and horses—are domestic. They give us food or work. Dogs and cats are domestic animals too. They give us love and friendship.

nocturnal: Animals that are active at night and at rest during the day. Nocturnal animals must be able to find food and to see their way in the dark. Owls, flying squirrels, and raccoons are nocturnal.

predator: An animal that hunts, kills, and eats other animals for food. Predators are not bad animals. Killing is simply their way of living. When a cat kills and eats a bird, it is acting as a predator.

prey: Animals that are hunted by other animals. Prey animals usually have ways to help protect themselves from being eaten. A bird may be a prey animal to a hungry cat.

virus: A tiny cell that lives inside other living cells and may cause illness. Viruses are so small they may be hard to see, even under a microscope.

591
Den

Dennard, Deborah

Do cats have nine
lives?

DATE DUE			